The Pulse of Our Times

(Witty Satires, Humour and Love)

Kuldip Salil

HIND POCKET BOOKS
An imprint of Penguin Random House

HIND POCKET BOOKS

USA | Canada | UK | Ireland | Australia
New Zealand | India | South Africa | China | Singapore

Hind Pocket Books is part of the Penguin Random House group of companies whose addresses can be found at www.hindpocketbooks.com

Published by Penguin Random House India Pvt. Ltd
4th Floor, Capital Tower 1, MG Road,
Gurugram 122 002, Haryana, India

Penguin Random House India

First published in Hind Pocket Books by Penguin Random House India 2019
This edition published in 2022

10 9 8 7 6 5 4 3 2

The views and opinions expressed in this book are the author's own and the facts are as reported by him which have been verified to the extent possible, and the publishers are not in any way liable for the same.

ISBN 9789353495381

Printed at Repro India Limited

www.penguin.co.in

FSC www.fsc.org MIX Paper from responsible sources FSC® C047271

This is a legitimate digitally printed version of the book and therefore might not have certain extra finishing on the cover.

HIND POCKET BOOKS

The Pulse of Our Times

Kuldip Salil was born in Sialkot in 1938, post-independence he settled in Delhi where he pursued his Masters in English literature and Economics from Delhi University. He retired as Associate Professor of English, Hans Raj College, Delhi University. An accomplished poet of Hindi, Urdu and English, he has published seven volumes of poetry. He is a recipient of numerous awards including the Sahitya Akademi Award for his works. He specializes in translating Urdu and Hindi poetry into English and vice-versa. He has translated works of eminent poets like Meer, Ghalib, Iqbal, Faiz and Faraz to name a few. His translation of Diwan-e-Ghalib received immense appreciation. His translation of Shakespeare, Wordsworth, Milton into Hindi was also well received. Presently, the poet is actively pursuing translation works and poetry.

To

Dear Anil and Ajay

Who

Left Us in Great Grief

Contents

Preface

Poetry in English, Hindi, Urdu and in other languages in translation has always been my first love, but the way I started writing a poem in English almost every week is quit interesting.

One day in January, 1998, I read a ten line poem on Sita Ram Kesri in Khushwant Singh's newspaper column. Kesri was the Congress president who had been dramatically removed by some Congressmen who wanted Sonia Gandhi to take over the reigns of the party. It was quite an amusing little poem. While reading the poem it occurred to me that perhaps I too could write in a similar vein. Accordingly, I sent two poems-one on J. Jayalalitha, and the other on Lalu Prasad Yadav – to Mr. Khushwant Singh. Jayalalitha, then the Chief Minister of Tamilnadu, had just celebrated her foster son's marriage, a very lavish affair on which she was said to have spent one hundred crore rupees. The source of this money was a subject of much chuckle and insinuations. Lalu Prasad on the other hand was jailed in the fodder scam and had just been released. He was as ever a colourful character and had entered into an electoral alliance with B.S.P.'s Kashi Ram. Both these pieces were in a comic-satirical vein. To my pleasant surprise both were immediately published – one in 'Malice Towards One and All' and the other in 'This Above All'. These columns are syndicated and are published in a large number of English and vernacular newspapers and journals across the country.

Thus began my journey with Shri Khushwant Singh, which is now in the sixteenth year. Although I had been writing poetry for forty years – occasionally in English but mainly in Hindi and Urdu – and had published five collections, it was this journey that took me finally into writing poetry in English on regular basis. And these poems form the bulk of poems selected for this volumes.

Written on almost every topic of general interest, these poems are a kind of commentary on the social-political-cultural scenario of the period. The range covered is wide. They were initially meant to be political satires. But as we went along, the subject varied from love poetry to sarcastic treatment of events. There are poems on celebrities who made news those days, on politicians-bureaucrats-businessmen nexus, personal poems of love and celebration, poems on social-political hypocrisy and on international events like Iraq war and the Taliban. If I am not being too presumptuous, this collection is cryptic history of the period and gives a bird's eye view of the political scene and the social scenario. Humour and irony are the defining features of these poems. I have selected about 125 out of some 400 poems contributed in the two columns. Of necessity – because space available in the newspaper is limited – these are small pieces of 15 to 20 lines mostly.

First and foremost, I am grateful to Mr. Khushwant Singh for finding these pieces worth publishing in his famed columns. He did not know me and I had never met him. Also I thank my colleagues and friends and my daughters Ritu and Sarika for their valuable suggestions. Thanks are also due to my friend Shri O.P. Sapra for his help in preparing the manuscript. Last but not the least I thank my publisher for bringing out the book in a short time.

– Kuldip Salil
1770, Outram Line, GTB Nagar,
Delhi – 110009 Mobile – 98100 52245

For Asha Bhonsle

(When she won Dada Saheb Phalke Award)

FIFTY-THREE YEARS and five thousand hits
Built on heartbreaks of initial years
What with a sister around, the empress great
And a whole crop of illustrious peers.
Was it versatility sheer?
Tragedy, comedy, cabaret, child-play
The songs of sadness, the numbers foot-tapping, the lyrics gay
The lilt, the mimicking, the sombre, the sunny
A voice of wine, a voice of honey
Vivacity, virulence, cut and shine.
A voice overflowing with vintage wine,
A voice all her own, a foil and a flail
To the supreme voice of the Nightingale
A voice of the young, a voice of the old
A voice that has a fold within a fold
A voice of tears, a voice to regale
A voice that is a sure card
A voice we especially hail
As it honours the top award.

10.10.2001

For My Grandchild

(On her first birthday)

I MAY or may not be around
When you come of age
And I really cannot presage
What future holds for you, at this stage.
But when I see the two little petals that they call your lips
And the angelic smile that floats like waves on a moonlit
stream,
The eyes that gleam and shoot their beam
Into my face,
A face like a budding rose
The naughty little nose,
A face that takes away the day's fatigue;
The eyes that mock at every intrigue,
The tiny legs and the little feet
And the joyous cackles that greet
My increasingly sober stance,
And, then, your spontaneous dance,
I must say whenever I see this paradisal state
I see the years ahead that await
You, and for your sake
I feel a kind of heartache.

15.6.2001

Stephen Hawking

(When the world famous scientist, who conquered all physical handicaps, was on a visit to Delhi)

WHEN THE wheeled chair moves through the city
From the Qutab to the Siri Fort hall,
When a bundled up so-called body
Holds in wonderment big and small,
When a permanently tilted neck props up a head
That overtops the skies high,
When a man about whom the doctors had said
That he would now any day die,
When a man with a paralysed body
Can take on Newton Einstein and the galaxy,
Can hold under his thumb all time and space,
Can pierce the black holes in the sky,
When a man who cannot utter a word
Can be impish, puckish, wittily naughty,
Can Celebrate life with sparkling humour,
Can be a world celebrity,
I stand up sky-high and salute the human spirit,
Its limitlessness, its might its grit,
The mind of man I sing
As I salute Stephen Hawking.

17.2.2001

New Year Resolution

In the new year, I'll so much increase my worth
That I'll be the richest man on earth
If you want to ask me how I will achieve this goal,
I'll kill my conscience and sell my soul,
I'll engineer bank fraud, commit robbery and
break Bill Gates skull
And thus become world's number one criminal;
Hopefully I'll head a flourishing political outfit
Which shares my noble mission, and then use it
To mislead the masses and fleece the nation;
I'll use my political clout to head the
Chamber of Commerce & Industry
Leave it free to hoard, evade taxes, get subsidy;
And thus siphon off the country's treasury;
Finally, lest somebody should steal,
My ultimate device I will not reveal;
And still if my plan is not perfectly laid;
I'll call upon the criminals of the world for help and aid –
In short,I will do my best
And leave it to God to complete the rest

22.1.2001

Age Of Violence

My dear young lady, you will be thrilled
For, if you refuse to marry your lover, you will be killed.
My dear teacher, learn to be mild
Never report against or rebuke a child
You had better save your life
For, in his books he might hide a knife,
My dear brother, take extra care
And never argue with your neighbour
Even if he usurps your house or parking space
Be good to him and sue for grace.
Let the motorists overtake you
Let them do whatever they do
Learn to be happy, learn to clap
Even when your son gives you slap
And if you are waylaid by a robber
Salute him and surrender
For, in this media age,
In this age of road rage
For, in this age of soaring violence
Even saving your life is an offence
Only your impotence is your defence.

18.3.2012

Remembering Faiz

ANNIVERSARY IT was, of birth or death, I knew not
Only the mind floated over moments and places,
I had with him known
Flooded with his ideas, his cold passion, his anguish dire,
And his hope with which I had from childhood grown,
Flooded over with sorrows ancient, suffering old
Of man, by man, for man,
His callousness, his cruelty massive, his suicidal stance.
And in a semi-trance
I see him in Rawalpindi Jail
Solitary, with the moon overhead and countless stars,
I see him in Beirut
Editing his journal in the midst of falling shells,
In Lahore, step out from 'koo-e-yaar' – his lover's lane –
To 'soo-e-daar', the hangman's noose,
I see him in Delhi, reading in a drone voice
'Aas us dar se tootti hi nahin
Ja ke dekha, na ja ke dekh liya,'
I see him drinking deep and long
Into the realms of beauty, love, equality,
Launching out into a land free from fantaticism
Leaping up barriers built with hate, for avarice, by hostility,
I see the subcontinent as one country,
And the world where romance embraces reality.

And suddenly, I hear a crash
And see a dream shattered not just a bit
And yet I see Faiz aglow
For poetry survives the poet
As his honest thought survives the man.

15.12.2001

Johnny Walker the Comedy King

(On his death)

"IT IS slow poison, give up drinking", said the doctor
"And, sir, who is in a hurry to die!"
Pat came the reply.
You never had a drop, and you were drunk
With joy, with good humour, with fun
For all the black poverty you went through early
You enriched with laughter every one.
Dead drunk by the roadside with a constable arguing,
"The earth is revolving, santri ji
So let me see you moving,"
Or tottering in the street with an empty bottle to beguile
A sight that made millions of people smile
Is no more, no more the age of laughter and fun:
Ponderous high seriousness, glum with 'wisdom' instead,
The age of innocence seems to be dead.
An era of insensitivity, when few would see
A joker incurable, or was it excess of grief
That in comedy found relief;
An era of prosperity, comfort and luxury
Becoming fast an era of tragedy
And now as you depart we'll miss forever

Johnny dear
Your age of randy laughter,
But before you board
How about one for the road?

28.8.2003

Our Mother Teresa

A woman not of miracles but a woman who was a miracle,
An angel of love, angel of beauty
Beautiful in service and spirit,
Beautiful in compassion and grit,
Lovely both in action and thought
Lovely for the suffering lot,
Ask the poor, sick and needy
And see their eyes lighting up,
The greatest Indian of the Century
Greatest in her utter humility;
Greatest in her services to humanity;
For, the lepers you and I would dread
These lepers the mother with her own hand fed,
O where in this world of 'me and mine'
Can you such a woman find !
A cancer patient was cured by her touch
And as such she is to be sainted,
Oh, a miracle has to be invented
For superstition is still the stuff
That the churches in their wisdom need
As if in this selfish world of greed
Service to man is not enough
As if a miracle is greater than the mother
As if sainthood can surpass her.

15.3.2003

M. F. Husain

(On his going in self-exile)

M. F. Husian is *no longer an Indian citizen*
What a great victory Indian democracy has won:
A shining example of artistic freedom
A tribute to our freedom of expression
Well done, my country, very well done
What need we poets and painters for
These sculptors, thinkers, writers all
Who show us the mirror and spade a spade call!
Nonsense
They do nothing except prick our conscience,
They are a burden on society that's why
We have hounded out Husain
And without a moral scar
Thrown him out away to Qatar.

9.10.2010

Ode to Benazir

Like for Cleopatra, Helen and Heer
I have a soft corner for Benazir.
After her father was murderd in a cell
Fightingly she went through hell.
Like a tornado then she rode to power
And started her own country to devour,
Treasure upon treasure
She stashed away
And bought herself a palace
In Surrey.
Surrounded by sycophants, cut
off from reality
The queen led merrily the
People's Party
Besieged, embattled, bruised and
Toiled
In thousand of crores is she now embroiled,
Corruption for politicians is such a necessity.
If proof is needed, this proves
Conclusively
How absolute power corrupts absolutely

Benazir: An Obituary

One more victim to terrorism,
One more martyr to democracy
Most ominously forewarned, a most courageous lady
Or shall we say, a nursling of tragedy
In line with the cursed families of the sub-continent
Snuffed out so violently!
Looked upon critically in her lifetime
Cut down cruelly in her prime
Highlighting the state of world,
So insecure and stark
She has left behind many a question mark:
Shall we ever learn from our tragic history
And root out from our midst fanaticism and bigotry!

2008

Welcoming Obama

(On his election in 2008)

BILL CLINTON or Bill Gates
I have never been a fan of the United States.
Bur Barrack Hussain Obama generates
Hopes of a new America, a new world order
Free from belligerent arrogance and Iraq-like disaster,
Free from racial hatred, downtrodden's misery.
Free from the scourge of terror, rule of the bully,
Free from "shameful" executives' lust and greed,
Their scandalous bonuses while the nation bleeds;
His heart is at the right place and his hand of friendship to
 the Muslim world;
Speaks of a vision, unimagined, unheard.
A breath of fresh air, a bit of a pleasing mystery,
Will Obama be a creator of history!

22.3.2009

Obama and Mayawati

A man can do what a man has done
How about a woman?
If he is not entirely black, she is not exactly white
If Obama is brilliant, Mayawati is naughty and bright
If he ousted high-end Hillary
She is taking on Mrs Gandhi
If he is calm and witty, she is catish and gritty
If he is a man of vision, creator of history
She is plotting dream victory
Because mainstream parties have failed the country
For the darkened community and
The downtrodden race
A minor revolution is taking place
So, the people of India, please mind
If Obama comes, Mayawati may not be far behind.

29.11.2008

The Kumbh

I have sinned all my life,
If you don't believe me ask my wife,
Indugled in treachery, lechery, fraud,
Ask my wife because she is a truthful lady
She'll tell you how I am mean and greedy
And now I have missed the one and only opportunity
Of washing my sins, as she has given me a slip
And along with Sushma Swaraj and Sonia Gandhi
Has gone to Sangam to have a
Holy dip
She is bound to rise politically
And become a minister, maybe
And be earthquake-free
While I stand here high and dry
And for at least twelve years cry
While she with all the past ones gone
Is free to commit any new sin
And once again the holy pardon win
And justify scoff
At the missed opportunity of her worse half,
Will you please speak on my behalf!

17.2.2001

Song of the New Millennium

LET THE wretched go to hell
And the weak jump into the well.
Let the sick sink and die,
In the new millennium
I have decided to fly high.
What are they to me those who starve
And those who shiver in the cold cold night?
How do I care for the jobless fools,
I want it all bright
With cabarets and cocktails.
The millennium great
I want to celebrate
In an intoxicated state.
Who is my neighbour? What is my brother?
I recognize none other
Than myself
With every gadget on my shelf.
In the new millennium to the brink
I want to be merry
And live only
To eat and drink.

8.1.2000

To Ghalib

(On his birth anniversary)

FOR THE sigh to be effective it needed an age
So, for the most part obscure you stayed,
Now, with the fool and the wise alike as you have become a
rage
And in your name now as fortunes are being made,
On this turning of the wheel
Tell me Mirza, how exactly you feel.
Do you still smart under the infamy, humiliation and hurt?
From your creditors are you hiding still?
What do you have to say
About the cliques and the patronage
Of your day and our age?
About your poetry's greatness
When there is universal 'yes'
I will only add my humble acclaim
And kiss your verses and your name.
But with these matters I'll some other time deal
For now, tell me pray: How do you feel?

16.1.1999

To Madhuri Dixit

(On her marrying an NRI surgeon)

HOW COULD you do it Madhuri?
India is a country of handsome men
Whom you have left sighing and sobbing
Brave and rich and sharp of ken
Droop, as their hands they wring.
Patriotism you lack and smack of foreign origin
O Madhuri why did you so many Indians shun
Fans who fawn on you and would gladly for your sake die
O curse be on you, you clever shrew
For an unknown, knife-wielding NRI
Not a pitying look you cast
And never for a moment thought
That as your wedding bells ring
Millions are losing heart
Among them, Hussain, Salil and Khushwant Singh.

20.10.1999

Higher Secondary Results

(An inspiring tale of a visually handicapped boy)

"HE SPREADS light in our lives," say his teachers.
Could there be a greater irony!
For, this young lad Laxman Mani
Running around from one end of the ground to the other
Overseeing every single game
With such high seriousness
In this vast tournament of fame
Is always full of laughter and often funny.
But today this boy, Mani, is to be found
Not just on this ground
But in the entire province
For, he is the prince
Over whom they all exult
For, he has topped today
This year's higher secondary result.
A poet, a debater and a cricketer
With visions of a future luminous
This boy, of course, of his own mind
He spreads light in our lives
This boy, who is by birth blind.

Meet my Mother

AFTER A goodly gap I met my mother
And I'm not going to eulogise her.
Aggressive, assertive, kindly, proud
Ruddy in complexion, eagle-eyed, the queenly mane
With a wave of hand who'd hold a crowd
And from a kilometer, you'd know
Her voice
Ringing aloud.
A female Buddha, cross-legged for
Seventy years
She sits in meditation, to let loose
On lesser mortals, as she finishes,
A spring-shower of soulful abuse
Whose domain is religion, politics,
morality
Hell and heaven, world and the country,
Brandishing her stick on every
"Obscene" scene
On the TV screen
Presiding over the kitchen from her
charpai
Breaking all rules, dietary.
A poet sans opportunity, headed for a century
Sending shivers down the spines of weaker members

Of the Family
Her only fault, as she puts her arm around my waist,
Towards me an ever indulging partiality.

To Sir Don Bradman

(On his death)

"SIR DONALD is dead."
My daughter said and became Sad
Sir DONALD at 92
Sir DONALD with whom
A century grew in batting
Sir Donald the king
Not only of hitting records out
of reckoning
Sir Donald of fair play
Of dedication, integrity
Sir Donald who pounded imperiously
Every loose delivery
In cricketing morality,
Poor Sir Donald who saw helplessly
The lepers of the world including his own country
What with paid defeat and counterfeit victory
Writing a new cricketing history.
She stood up to go as she said:
"The age of romance and chivalry is dead."

23.3.2001

India's Hope

(When a eunuch won election to the Madhya Pradesh Assembly)

YOU ARE proud of your manhood
And you, your womanhood flaunt
We gave you fifty years to come good
And if you want
We can give you a few more
To explore your powers of heart, head and soul
And into a ball roll
All your strength and energy and will
To fulfill the promises each one of you makes;
Otherwise you must know
We have very high stakes
In the future of this country;
And don't tell us we didn't warn you,
Though for now, it is one assembly seat in M.P.
That a eunuch has won,
At this rate, very easily
We'll take over the entire country
For if you fail
What's now a wind will become a gale
Eunuchs of the country, unite
The time has come to show your might.

22.4.2000

Mallika-e-Tarannum

(On Noorjahan's passing away)

"Music is my God," she said
And raised quite a storm
For the fanatics of course
It was anti-Islam
For the frayed nerves of the subcontinent
Her music was a healing balm.
The ring in her voice is indeed her own
The melody that moves even a stone
Except, of course if it is a Taliban.
'Mujh se pehli si mohabat mere Mahboob na maang'
For one, when she sings Faiz
We know what she sings and she alone has :
The magic that music and poetry work.
But when the Lashkar breaches
The Red Fort
And Musharraf blows hot and cold
I don't know who should be told
That with Noorjahan gone
Another bridge is broken
Between India and Pakistan.

15.12.2005

Bhagat Singh's Lament

You know my motherland is
dear to me,
And I am ever present here;
When the hangman's rope was
put around my neck
I stopped him a while, to declare
Something, which now with
you I share:
My heart, my head, my body, my soul
All those of my comrades as a whole
Will be but seed from which will sprout
A proud nation of people,
Happy and free
A country of prosperity, equality opportunity
A resplendent India, jewel of the world
On your behalf my country-men, dear
I gave a solemn word.
But today what I see, what do I see...?
O' let me not cry,
I will never cry,
I will rather die
Again, and again, and again....

30.3.1998

To Sir Veerappan

(The Southern bandit who remained at large for years)

FOR YOUR fearlessness, for your courage
For your intelligence, for your stratagem
For the way you play with the bureaucrat and the politician
For your ability to hold states to ransom,
We the crooks and cowards of India
Salute you, Sir Veerappan.
But why should you hide from anyone?
Come out of the forest and end your quest.
For here, you know, most of the powerful men
Are your brethren,
Over whom, for the range and depth of your experience
And your moustache, the pride of this nation
You can easily be the sovereign.
And for this suggestion, dear bandit
Take me under your protection.

8.6.2001

He too is an Indian

AN APPARITION, a ghost or a spectre seeing
How can I call him a human being?
Sunken cheeks, slumping face,
Bones and bones in its place
Protruding high, and the sinking eye,
The hair of grass, untended, dry,
The trunk half sunk, the back and belly
I cannot, but can you see?
The legs bent double, the chin on the knees,
He is a human, he too is an Indian, please;
He sees the sky, he looks at the earth
From them perhaps he'd like to know his worth
For he knows what his country will say,
He is not worth a meal a day,
For he is worse than rats whom it can feed
And throw the surplus in the ocean indeed.
He has seen his son and wife collapse
But he'd survive them all perhaps
For this country is after all his
For he is really what India is.

27.4.2001

Crime and Politics

IT'S MEAN of me, mean of us all
To grudge them at all their rightful place
They, the truly democrats
And we, the ones lacking in grace,
For they are the people's men who work in the fields.
They rape, we gape
They murder, we demur
They kidnap, smuggle and blackmail,
We quail
They are the men of conviction
We, of contradiction
They reflect and defect
Get respect, money and ministry
We crib and envy;
But we are learning quickly,
For as they fleece, exploit and cheat
We fold our hands and fall on their feet.
Men of action, gifted, fearless, free
They'll tackle corruption, pollution, prudery
Tackle Pakistan, remove poverty
And as we whitewash history
A bright future awaits the country.

23.3.2001

Diwali

SINCE IT is a festival of light,
Of victory of good over evil
Naturally, every heart in India is bright
With joy, with hope, with goodwill.
Not a soul will sleep on empty stomach now
Nor will anybody shiver out in the cold
Nobody will commit suicide for debts
Nothing will be now in the black market sold.
Since Ram has come home
All hoarders from the country will flee,
It is not mere bursting of crackers
It is the death knell of adulterators
Of pulses and ghee,
And the end of moral poverty.
The exploitation of man by man now
Will be a matter of history.
The big will, of course, feel big
But so will the small,
It is not a small thing, dear countrymen
It is Ramrajya after all.

6.11.1999

A Paradise, that's Delhi

HUMPTY DUMPTY, hocus pocus, hurly burly
If there is a paradise on earth, it is Delhi
Full of people, overflowing
Markets onto the road going
Full of fumes, full of gases
Full of ultra modern asses
Full of shining, made-up faces
Full of heart and cancer cases
Car and truck and motorcycle
Full of vehicle on the vehicle
Full of jolting, full of stoking
Full of lanes and bylanes choking
Full of housing haywire going
Full of sewage into Jamuna flowing
Full of callous indifference breeding
Full of pastures fast receding
Full of power, and still power crisis
Full of smoothly rising prices
Full of girth and grime and mirth
Our Delhi is a paradise on earth.

14.4.2007

Twinkle, Twinkle Little Star

(When nursery rhymes were sought to be Indianised)

You have twinkled enough, o little star
Your hour has come now to pack up and go
Our own sun has risen already, and so.
All western light from the eyes of mother India
We must pull out and in the ocean throw.
And you Baa Baa Black sheep
You are not a sheep but a vulture,
A wolf in sheep's clothing, who'll eat up
Our centuries old solid culture!

21.7.2006

Meet my Wife

A DELICATE person is to be handled with care
And when it's a wide-eyed wife, elusive and fair
One should invoke the gods repeatedly
And then alone dare.
Sweet and fair, sour, and a tower of strength
For my frailty to lean loosely about,
Whispering aloud, equal to a crowd, mild and proud
Loud and low, in quick turn, soft and stout,
And almost ever, ready for a bout,
But I write this because I have no doubt
That but for her, this candle would have long been out.
Existing on her bounty, utterly oblivious of the world, a free bird,
Free to follow my fancy,
Free to fly on the wings of poesy,
Free from seeing the children off to school,
Buying spices, looking after the meter and the motor.
If I'm free from futility, social senility
It's because I'm lucky;
A buffer between me and strife, a policy for life,
If even these days I can manage to look sunny
It is because she bears with me even when I'm funny
And if you don't tell her, the rhyme you read
Is possible because of her, indeed.

24.11.2001

Hurrah for Indian Police

In Delhi, crime is down, says the
Commissioner
One cheer, A Happy New Year;
Three terrorists escape recently
In this safe, safe city,
The biker gangs are all but gone, robberies decline
Rapes are unheard of, women feel fine
Bedecked with gold, they go out
And dine
Well done, sir, A Happy New Year.
And the second cheer
Goes to Rathore the protector
Of a young girl's life and honour –
Wonderful sir, A Happy New Year.
And the third cheer goes to a
Mumbai Deputy Commissioner of
Police and his junior
For dancing with Chhota Rajan's gangster,
Thus ensuring that they keep awake at night
And give the crime world a mortal
fright –
You are our saviour,
Great going, dear, A Happy New Year.

25.10.2009

I Love My India

While the country experiences prosperity
Society is evolving, spirituality spreading
Alongwith ethics and morality
Giving a fillip to feelings of kindness, love and sympathy-
Except that a maid in the house is beaten blue and black
Except that she is branded and kept hungry-
To learn a little more humility;
Except that minor girls are sold out in prostitution -
For thorough education;
Except that cut-off for admission flies to the skies
Except that the suicides rise
Except that inequality increases with every reform
Except that an MLA on horseback rides to the railway
    platform
Except that patriotism has a new definition
Which is competition in corruption -
Dignity equality fraternity are to us a religion,
We love our country, we're proud of our nation.

Money and Murder

Which car is better, that was the matter
And there was a murder;
Let your heart not sink
But you can die, if you fail to supply
Money to buy a drink;
Be a reasonably dependable mouse
And allow your son to sell your house,
Let you your father's funeral skip
But never postpone your daughter's outstation trip.
I'll tell you how to make money, come —
Kidnap a classmate and earn a ransom,
Money makes the mare go
So kill anybody and into the river throw,
Smuggle opium and sell your nation's secrets,
Or whatever else the means
Let no scruples be seen
Nowadays all money is clean.

Talibans All

IF YOUR faith is blind
And you are senile in the mind
You will find with God's grace
That the world is a wonderful place.
If you can fell and kill
An infidel at will.
If you can hide your women underground
And be culturally pure and sound
You are definitely jannat bound.
So we too have decided to thrash
A birthday or a New Year bash
And slay
The Valentine's Day.
And crash into every honeymooner's bed
Lest it should be said
That they have built a heaven on earth
And we have lagged behind.
So from today; while we embrace the USA
No 'hello', no 'hi!'
We ban all merriment, all joy.
And be one up with the Taliban State
To make our Bharat once again great.

10.5.2001

Whistle Blower

(When a district collector was shot dead
by the oil mafia)

There used to be in Lakhanpur Kheri, UP, a Manjunath
Who richly deserved the oil mafia's wrath
For preventing them from committing robbery
Continually and openly;
And what else could that mafia do
If Manmad Additional district collector too Into a fit of rage
flies
And obstructs their honest enterprise,
Except set him aflame
Because that's the rule of the game,
And why should one per cent of the bureaucracy
Be a black sheep to its fraternity
And question the integrity
Of the mining mafia, blackmarketeer and the adulterator;
How can anybody be a whistle blower
And escape murder!

10.5.2001

India Against Corruption

The crowds half a kilometre long;
That at Anna Hazare rallies throng;
Are obviously mistaken and wrong;
Thousands of men, women and children;
When they raise slogans to say in unison;
"Down, down, down with corruption;"
When they say to get any work done;
However fair;
They have to grease the palm everywhere;
When they resent massive capitation fees
And the way the officials fleece;
When they cry, how for the people minus the privileged and the elite;
It is becoming difficult to make both ends meet;
They are obviously wrong;
Because our GDP is going strong;
Led by the oldest political party;
When our entire political fraternity;
BSP, SP, BJP, NCP;
Is against corruption and bribery;
How can there be any corruption in the country?
So even when his supporters are a billion strong;
Anna Hazare will continue to be wrong.

3.7.2011

End of the World

My friend and foes, my wealth and property, all my worry
My life from end to end, my heart-breaks, my glee,
The defeats I suffered, my sought – after victory
These flickering light, in a river floating free,
The works I could produce and the books that couldn't the
light of the day see –
For me the world would end when I cease to be.
But O, if I die young. If I am taken away in the flush of my
act –
If I am cut in the middle with swelling sobs around,
With the tears that fill the burial ground
And with all my treasures yet to be found !
Just then I hear a sound:
Nature will shower its holy grace,
And people better than me
Will fill my place.

17.5.2011

Temple Treasure

(When a huge treasure was found in a temple in Kerala)

Temples are houses of prayer, piety and God
But you have to secure the future of the Lord
With heaps of rubies, piles of gold
And glittering diamonds, centuries old,
For which the poor village folk
And the people of the town
Must die of hunger
With disease be down
While the priests and trustees of the kingly treasure
Their share in it do solemnly measure
And should a Sai Baba or a Bhagwan
After a painful disease be gone,
An honest age of loot is automatically switched on
O the silly people do not know the worth
Of these messengers of God on this wretched earth
Until they accidentally reveal their divinity
And are found to have millions and billions in their kitty.

9.6.2011

To Pakistan with Love

(On Pak foreign minister Hina Khar Rabani's visit to India)

We love Pakistan for her Foreign Minister, if for nothing else
And the lovely smile on a lovely face that she could bring,
Her manner sincere, her straight talk, her movements
smooth.
And in spite of Pakistani media's gibberish uncouth,
She is hopefully the face and voice of Pakistan's maturity and
youth.
The fanatics who would object to her Birkin bag
And in entire womankind find a snag,
The same fanatics in colour whatever, anywhere
Should be declared as diggers of grave
Not only of peace and prosperity
But of their community, religion and country.
Forgive them, O Lord, for they know not what they say,
Perhaps their upbringing teaches them to bite and bray!

Happy New Year

Free from the vanities of the world,
Free from the quirks of life,
Free from our follies absurd,
Free from ignoble strife,
Free from worry, free from fear,
A Happy New Year to you, my dear,
Free from the dry tap, free from the power cut
Free from the telephone dead, free from a tyre phut,
Free from the officials' arrogance, free from a friend's pretence,
Free from a cantankerous neighbour, free from a faithless lover,
Free from a leader's cut, free from a policeman's butt
Free from insensitive law, free from the inflated bill,
Free from a swollen eye, free from the sleeping pill,
Free from a made-up face, free from the mad, mad race,
Full of bounty, full of grace
Of sunny days and nights clear.
A Happy New Year to you, my dear.

10.1.2006

Becoming Rich

Why not become rich overnight;
And lead a life, lavish and bright
For which there are opportunities galore
For instance, on paper build a colony
Or float a fake company
And run away with the needy
And greedy people's money
And like Bacha, the A. Raja aide;
Be in murder or suicide paid
Ours is a free country;
So it is great opportunity;
To use scam or bribery;
And climb atop the fortune's tree;
It is time that the swindlers of the country unite;
And for their statues in Sansad Bhawan fight;
For, they are God's chosen creation;
And the builders of a great nation.

17.4.2011

Grow up, Folks

(On Adarsh scam when flats meant for Kargil widows were syphoned off by politicians, bureaucrats and military officers)

Maligning our businessmen, contractors and the bureaucracy
Eternally questioning our honesty
I don't know why our people are getting crazy leaders'
2G spectrum, Sukhna land deal and Adarsh in Mumbai
Speak only of the leaping economy of a dynamic country
Be fair, before you declare
Don't be churlish and mean
Were Commonwealth Games not absolutely clean?
And by giving the rules a new interpretation
And accommodating honest CMs
Brave generals and many a noble civilian
Has Adarsh Society not done proud to the nation,
Giving the Kargil heroes a cause for exultation?
What if the Kargil widows cry?
And their, old parents die?
Every single segment of public life reeks of corruption;
Don't despair that nothing can be done
Be a yogi and from the burning pyre
Extract some fun.

29.1.2011

Fair Prices

I have been all over the town
Met the king and the clown
Don't be despondent, do not frown
The prices of essentials will come down;
Be it vegetable, fruit or tea
Or the price of transport, tuition fee
Or humble jaggery, pulses or ghee
The prices are headed fast to a level
Where they are fated to be;
A level that Pawar wills and for which
The traders love to hoard
But you and I cannot afford;
But what of that?
Eating will only make you fat;
So do not take a view, low and dim
Fast, instead, three days a week
And remain handsome and slim.

5.2.2011

Astrology and Joshiji

(When Astrology Was Sought to be Taught as a Subject at the University)

NOW YOU'LL be able to know years in advance
Whether your daughter will marry in Bhagalpur or France,
Whether your son'll become a doctor or a philosopher
Or, stars favouring, a flourishing astrologer,
When your neighbour-woman is going to have labour pains,
By how much is the stock market going to crash,
You'll know – in a flash
The year and the month and the day of your luck
When you'll make a fast buck,
How faithful your future wife will be,
Your children will know years in advance
When you'll die
And plan accordingly.
It is the proudest science of the 21st century
Congratulations, Dr Joshi,
For introducing it at the university
It is bound to remove ignorance and illiteracy,
Only a professor of physics could have done it
Through his bum-chum
Dr – a medical doctor – H. Gautam

5.5.2001

The Smiling Buddha

(When the Talibans in Afganistan pulled down the world famous statue of Lord Bhuddha)

"When tanks and rockets and the bullets –
Hit me even in stone and granite,
When fuming fury in a state of fit
Turns to use the dynamite
When frenzy, violence, vengeful wrath –
The proud progeny of Satan supreme
And their kinsmen intolerance, hate
Howl and growl and loud scream
With all the self-righteous sounds,
I sit, as I did, under the Bodhi tree
Though, distracted for a while
And, as is my wont, for centuries now
I quietly smile.
But oh! the hunger stalks the blighted land
And bitter chill rips the bones apart,
But oh: the children in their thousands die
And under their veils the women cry
And the powers that bred the Talibans
Now hypocritically sigh,
I must confess I am distraught
Do I still smile?"

3.2.2001

Crorepati

"I REMAIN a superstar
Of yesterday, today and tomorrow
Only, I have declared a small war
On a minor sorrow.
An angry young man who became an MP
And landed up in the ABC,
And because I love the people so much
I have decided to make them crorepati.
Daily
I invite them openly
To switch off all other channels
And play with me alone on the TV.
I am not making anybody greedy
I only invite the needy
No, no, the greed I never stir
Nor am I making anybody gambler
Rather, engaging the whole nation
In a fruitful occupation:
I am people's man after all
And willing to play any role, big and small,
Not at all, by no stretch of imagination
Is it a fall."

3.11.2000

Miss World

MY HEART leaps up whenever I hear
That an Indian girl has made it to the top of the world.
Shyly and blushing I stand before a mirror
And congratulate myself that I am running only
in my fifty-third.
I comb my hair afresh and straighten my back
And as I swell my chest with half shut eyes
The entire country I surmise
And to my delirious-delight discover
That I am the best of guys.
Profound praises to the Indian beauty does my heart sing
And from another world do the bells in my ears ring,
Proud and only fifty-three
As I stand in a state of ecstasy
I feel somebody pull at my shirt and say quietly,
Are you sleeping dadaji?

2001

The Power of Money

THE RIGHT to booze, the right to brawl
The right to abuse one and all
And if you deny my wish, block my route
It is my natural right to shoot.
I dance naked, I dance drunk
On the bonnet, on the roof of a car,
In the middle of the road I molest
I am the rising star.
I shake the earth when I drive
Run for your life if you can
I knock you down because I know
Dead or alive, I can buy any man.
An MP's son, a minister's nephew
The kin of an admiral, a tycoon's relation
Nothing can you do to me,
You ninety-nine per cent people
Of this nation.

Higher Telephone Tariff

(When telephone tariff was hiked under Jag Mohan)

HELLO, O it is you, dearest,
I know the world is bad
I know you are alone
I know the weather makes you sad
I know you expected me to phone;
I know the maid has not come again
I know the grocer overcharged
Oh that headache again
I know the man just barged
Into our flat last night
I know that the taps have gone dry
I know that you want to cry,
I know you love me a lot
I know, I know it, sweetheart,
If there is anything other than this to say
Say it, otherwise put down the receiver, pray,
I am sorry to deny you even this little comfort or fun
But dearest Suman,
Blame me not for this,
Blame Jagmohan.

2.7.2000

The Great Cricket Bazaar

More than a lakh of rupees for every run he scores
Dhoni has been sold for six crores
For every ball he bowls, Young Ishant Sharma too
Will get a lakh or more.
So why should not every street turn into a pitch
And urchins score boundaries by breaking our windows and
doors?
Why should they pore on books of drab Chemistry,
Study dull Mathematics, rotten History?
Rather than concentrate on silly mid-on!
And why should they play foot-ball or hockey
And not become a batsman of the off side?
As the grand auction opens a floodgate
Even though retired already, it is not too late,
Come what may, I must keep fit and stout
And start hitting right and left before I am out.

16.3.2008

Old-age Romances

(When there was a buzz that the Russian President, Putin was marrying again)

The more he says 'no' the more it is 'yes'
And you are quite right in your guess
It is President Putin that I have in mind
For, if the French does it, can Russians be far behind?
And with Vidya Naipaul and Salman Rushdie
Going about with second, third and fourth beauty
And Chancellor Kohl remarrying after eighty,
Among the celebrities of every kind and country
It is now almost becoming a rage
To have an armcandy in old age -
And because the trend is set by what the celebs do,
I see some hope for myself too.

6.8.2008

Play on

(On Hindi film songs)

From the shadows of the evening till the break of dawn
Music being the soul of life, play on
Play on because it'll fill you with love and praise,
Play on because it will illuminate your gaze
Play on if you want to soothe your sullen soul
Play on if solace and joy be your goal,
Play on to the cruel and the coward because music can
Melt a monster into human and mould a human into man.
Play on to the whole nation the universal melody
For what has kept this country together chiefly so
Is nothing lofty
But the good old and the humble Hindi film songs
Play on, for Tamil Nadu enjoys it
And Assam understands it every bit:
"Ae meri zohra jabin, too abhi tak hei hasin aur mein jawan"
Play on, for the Kargil men and patently hostile to Hindustan
Even Musharraf succumbs to the magic of old Hindi songs
A bond still between India and Pakistan.

9.6.2001

The Golden Cup

(When India won the cricket world cup in 2011)

Beaming, booming, bursting
Dancing wild with joy, with tails up
Hurrah: We have won the World Cup
Night turns into day and the day into eternity
For once casteless, creedless with just Indian identity
A billion plus people become a fraternity.
Ah this rarest of the rare unity,
A madness in which every beggar is a king.
And from coast to coast
Indian is the world's toast
Is it not time now that everything else should go to hell
And we eat cricket, drink cricket and live under its spell
Time that with wealth and glory
These heroes are fed so wantonly
That they become two quintals fat and ten feet tall
And into a lengthy slumber fall!

17.4.2011

A Visit to Pakistan

(On the occasion of Indo-Pak cricket match in Lahore)

SMILES, SPREAD on jalebis and kababs
Greet us, and a Pathani suit is sold at half the price
A firm handshake, a feeling warm and nice
For a bye-bye, and amazement and delight
In our heart
At what it is and what we had thought.
And the grey old man with sunken eyes
Hugs me to his heart and cries
As I mention my grandpa's name
In our ancestral street in downtown Lahore;
A dozen doors open, and faces a score or more
Glow at the sight of an old Lahori;
And instantly, I see our two armies on the border arrayed
I see our leaders on the podium high
And hear loud slogans with arms upraised
Taking a vow to finish the foe, or die;
And I see at Gaddafi Stadium the incredible sight –
In the midst of cheers, long and loud
I see the tricolour fluttering proud;
And as the reel move fast
I see the story in both its parts –
And as we win the series they win our hearts.

7.8.2004

Football and War

(On the occasion of football world cup in 2002)

WHILE THE world goes nuts and the crowds do the wave,
While the young and not-so-young and the old and more old
Rhyme and rotate and rave,
While Europe is aglow, Africa is full flow
And Latin America is the prince of the show
And Asia plays the host,
While every foot is above the ground, every foot is kicking around
And the world is in cheering drowned,
While colours fly and the skies are lit
And the world is in a frenzied fit
Of joy, of hope, of pride,
We in India and Pakistan slide
Towards a mutually assured annihilation.
And rather than feeling a sense of shame
That, while Senegal defeats the world champion
And Cameroon emerges world power.
We are nowhere in the game,
Rather than feeling a sense of shame
We talk fanaticism, shun sanity, live medievally,
Justify our jehadi mentality,
And are ever itching for a fight
If somebody tells us, it's silly,
For ours is the only religion and wisdom is our monopoly.

6.7.2002

Beating England in England

CHAUVINISM IS bad, and euphoria is not good always
But they can sometimes raise
The dwindling spirit, the crashing morale
And in no small measure, if they don't make us vain
Can help us stand up again.
So if Ganguly took off his shirt and ran around the ground
So if they kissed and embraced one another
Like Columbus's men when they had at last found
So if they kissed and embraced all night into the dawn
It was really and truly on.
So if the whole nation goes delirious for a while
And the sick and the solitary also smile
It was not just because we had beaten England in England
But beaten in style
For it was not just a mountain of a score
More important, the top order was there no more
More important, it was by Kaif, Yuvraj and Harbhajan
That the deed was done;
The divisive brigades of our country, to please note,
That at the moment in however insignificant a way
We stood as a nation
Tall and proud, varied and one
With our youth reaching out to the sun.

3.8.2002

No Cartoons, Please

(When first Mamta Bannerjee and then the central government banned cartoons in journals and books)

Ladies and gentlemen, can I ask a simple question
Why should anybody laugh, why should there be any fun
Why should we enjoy a joke, why see a comedy
Why must feel happy and easy,
And why should we forget, laughter is a disease
If you laugh, your blood pressure will increase.
No butter, no sugar, no meat, no cheese
And certainly no laughter, please!
Wit and humour cause peptic ulcer
If you don't believe me, ask your doctor,
And smiles annoy friends, smiles are enemy of the people
Why should people be so irresponsible
And not remain serious and dull?
It is time, we changed our constitution
Ban this silly thing, called freedom of expression
Remove all cartoons from newspapers and journals
And in the supreme interest of the nation
Ban all wit, humour and fun.

11.12.2012

Budget Blues

JUGGLERY OF figures, jungle of facts
Thousands and thousand crores of money,
Tempting and teasing, a nice mess
Of sugar-coated pills, of sour honey
Causing a collapse, raising a hiss,
That makes many a one his heartbeat miss,
The jumping frog, the thumping chest
Hoping for the status quo, and for the rest
Innovative ideas, initiative bold
Sops that leave the people cold
The old complain, the young ignore
As figures burn and thumbs are sore.
More and more of learned debate
Crushing a mortal under its weight
An instrument of our annual fate
Comes to haunt us and our aunt
Whether we want or do not want.
A feather in the cap of those in charge
Of no concern to masses at large,
It is indeed a document great
If-you are free from a nervous trait;
But I should thank it rather than curse
It doesn't as yet tax my verse.

15.3.2003

In Praise of War

(When coalition war planes bombed Iraqi cities)

A WELL-illuminated city, extremely well
Lit up on the roof-top, twigs of the tree and the market place
Leaping into life at midnight or hiding its head at high noon
As the houses sob and the cattle swoon
As the street collects a pile
Courtesy a freedom-filled missile,
As hospitals swarm and towns empty
Leaving behind the old to oversee
Its reconstruction into a town of liberty
Courtesy precision action and masterly technology.
In this meantime, it all can dip and disintegrate
In the meantime, it can rely entirely on its fate
Seeing. far into the sky for peace and mercy
And the future that is to be
Courtesy the Coalition bombs of universal liberty,
Courtesy the burning passion of the Coalition
To burn all that it doesn't like, and refashion
The world into a free and democratic village
Under its direct tutelage,
To refashion the world into god's own place
Under its own law of boundless grace
Where oil and power and wood and stone
Will hopefully be all its own.

27.7.2003

US Case on Iraq

(George Bush speaking)

UN? WHAT UN? Nonsense
I am, I alone am, and hence
A million deaths, devastation etc, only show
How Important is my defence.
Rest of the world, Russia China, Germany, France,
What's this, their silly stance
And I really cannot understand
The behaviour of those made of clay and sand;
Don't they know for their very survival
They must to my tune dance?
These demonstrations world wide, this hue and cry
Why on earth, why, and why?
This Robin Cook, only a cook
But with Tony Blair as an obedient ally
What more do I need, how care I!
The two of us in military boots
Will tell the world we care two hoots
The two of us will prove by far
That the war we fight is a just war
The two of us will prove as we jointly fight
That the law of the jungle is once again right.

29.3.2003

In Praise of an Ass

I cannot praise you for want of words
I can only worship you for what you are,
Our honour, our glory, the heart beat of the nation
You are, for one, our cricketing star;
For another, so gentle, so docile, so mild
Anybody can flog you, even a child,
Such patience as only you possess
Humiliation you alone can stomach
We salute you for in this you represent our people
And their unshakable faith in superstition and luck.
Night and day, regularly you bray
And we cannot tell the one from the other
So sweet, so promising in the same old noises
That you are truly our natural leader.
O ass dear, 1 fear, I cannot measure up
To your worth, your greatness, your qualities of heart and
mind,
The wisdom you have and we only toil to find:
This is even when I myself am a natural ass,
But never mind, others will make up the loss
And like you start eating grass.

7.7.2003

Saddam and I

I WOULD never be Saddam, I do not know about you,
And if I ever were I would never do.
First the deeds of a wolf and then be a rat
To be tied by the tail and taken to the streets of the world.
A butcher and warmonger, a man of endless bluster
I would never be, and if I ever were
I would never have my men slain, my sons killed
And still gone on creeping in a hole...
A thousand bullets would be through my head before I got
caught
By God I would have fought like mad and never lent lustre
To the deeds of a mad invader;
O the man is psychotic for what he has done
He is surely another American.

6.2.2004

India Shining

(On the eve of general election 2004)

FROM MORN to mid-day and evenings often
With buckets and brushes beside
A long row of them I see
Waiting anxiously to wash your house white, to paint it bright;
From unknown villages they hail, to many a shut factory belong
And have worked hard and long
And now they are pining,
My India is shining.
I see a tea garden on the TV
And a hundred workers, more ghosts than men,
I see a shop sleeping, customers empty
And the shopkeeper understanding,
A dispensary dilapidated, a primary school shut
And on the wall beside, I see a hung poster
Broad and bright in smile
Meant for the voter,
I can see precisely the 'feel-good factor;'
In the meantime, my electricity bill is up three hundred per cent
And I am quietly whining,
My India is shining.

5.4.2004

God and the Flood

A WHOLE city dies by water
And the sea lies where it was not
Nor was it the tourists' lot
To see their homes and hotels again;
Perhaps it was a sinful city
But was there nobody, just nobody
Good and pure and holy
To deserve His mercy?
Or is it that God is good at writing tragedy
More than comedy?
Does he kill children and afflict the noble souls most
grievously
Or crush everybody to stand further tall?
Does he exist at all,
Or is He our emotional necessity?
Perhaps, he is a slave of the karma theory,
I cannot argue, and logic will not do
But what do we do of the mystery
For on it rests seemingly
More harm than good that religion does
And the conduct of humanity,
What do we do if it teases naggingly!

6.2.2005

Tsunami and the Rest

WHITE AND black, forth and back
A three-storeyed flood enters the bedroom
And swallows up a five-star situation
As also the habitation of the wretched of the coast,
Leaving behind bodies of all sizes and condition,
Bodies of children without parents, parents without children
Bodies of husbands single, bodies of wives alone
And the rest are left to mourn
On the beach, and far, far away from the sea's reach.
Cots and cottages collide with cars
And future meets a blank horizon
As shanties and bungalows submerge
And sing a dirge on human situation,
Its brittleness, its unbidden fate
And the huge uncertainty of the human state;
A lament on the callousness of the impersonal universe,
And still, I cannot get rid of my personal fears, my penny
    fears
And rather than live today
Plan my misery for unborn years.

16.1.2005

Ode to Spring

A pall of gloom descends on the earth
What with personal tragedies, national sorrow and woes of
the world
What with a thick dense fog blocking the eye
And passing into the mind unobstructed.
A winter of cosy comfort, no
A winter of chilling bones awaits
A flowery field, a yellow mustard ocean, and a fragrant breeze,
A cold winter awaits warmth in the heart,
A cooing of the cuckoo and a corresponding melody on our
lips unborn, unbidden,
And some rosy news of men becoming honest, women safe,
children carefree
And God kind,
It awaits under thy impact, some fresh blood, a change of
heart, a new mind,
O spring
I see you are already smiling,
Keep smiling on us, and as you come face to face
Not on our fond and foolish hope, O!
Keep showering on us your bounty and grace

4.4.2005

Rising Taxes, Soaring Bills

BATHING IS a dirty habit, and washing, a superstition deep
Avoid them, but still if you must,
Jump in a well or in a river leap
And within your budget keep,
For, water is life, and life is no longer cheap.
Use no fan, light not your house at night
It's much better to have inner light
And keep the heart cheerful and eyes bright.
Keep no vehicle, buy no petrol
For, good health should be your goal,
For which walk to and fro
Or better, do not anywhere go.
And if you don't want to starve, or be out in the cold
Take my advice, and don't grow old,
For, on your savings and interest thereon
Whatever exemption existed, is quietly gone.
This globalised country needs you no more
So the FM most graciously shows you the door.
So cheer you up, for, it's a wonderful situation
Because higher the taxes, greater the nation.

21.5.2005

Tale of Two Ambanis

Great are the ways of God, and greater still
Are our friends Mukesh and Anil
Owning between them a mere one lakh crores
They love each other, and I am sure, they would have loved
    better if they had a little more.
Itching for a complete control or the biggest slice
The two are a model of sound business sense and sacrifice
Free from personal ego and power lust
They put their family and the nation first,
Pillars of the country's economic health
They make their shareholders hold their breath;
Knowing the role of their mood and mentality,
Knowing that the country watches the changing position
Of their eyebrow
They act with grace and responsibility,
Only occasionally
To keep the brotherly love burning bright
The two Ambanis openly fight.

4.6.2005

Greatest Leader

(On the occasion of non-violent revolt in Tunisia and Egypt in 2011)

For all the pomp and show;
Gandhi died in India long ago;
And we would never know;
His greatness, till the aliens were to declare;
That he is of all times the greatest leader;
Until Egypt were to rise en masse;
And Tunisia a threshold cross
Peacefully to usher in democracy.
We love him, by him swear;
And day and night sing his prayer;
But never our assets truthfully declare.
True followers of his philosophy
We never indulge in corruption,
Practice bribery;
Not only do our politicians live poorly
Our traders serve only their country;
Even an IAS couple collects five hundred crore only;
So as long as the sun rises,
Piercing the cloud
We will do Gandhi proud.

26.3.2011

Ram Rajya is Here

(When an MLA slapped a policeman and another allegedly killed an engineer in UP)

Where service to the people is a religion
And every meeting ends with Jan Gan Man,
Mayawati's party has no criminals, not even one.
This is something only by her rivals done.
No Minister or MLA can
Slap a common citizen or a policeman
Nor kill a Commissioner or engineer
For not collecting enough money for the Chief Minister
On her epoch-making birthday,
Nor his hand on a poor woman lay
But if one does come his way
He neither rapes nor molests ever
And if still she creates a stir,
He arranges a jail term for her -
Thus for every criminal UP is a terror
A model of law and order,
It is a State where Ram, Lakhshman
run factories and schools
And Sita Mata herself rules.

12.3.2011

Earthquake and After

(Earthquake in Pak occupied Kashmir in 2005)

I DON'T know whether Musharraf' s offer of open LOC is
genuine or not,
I don't know whether India's offer of help and helicopters
Is also with political grandstanding fraught,
I don't know whether the biggest tragedy in Pakistan's history
Will even slightly change their jehadi mentality,
But I do know that a hundred thousand are dead already
And more will die of cold shortly or starve
Because killing, and not living, is our first preference
And Pakistan spends 60 per cent of its budget on defence.
Of course, we're negotiating, and we'll negotiate
And ultimately the aid will reach at any rate
But the 'ultimate' will depend on the victims' fate.
I think, it will take the two countries a few more earthquakes
Before, in peace and cooperation, they realise their stakes.

11.4.2005

Sporting Nation

(When our sports scene was dismal)

IN ATHLETICS, we make big news –
For drug abuse;
In hockey, we are ruling the world
By standing 23rd,
In the line of Dhyan Chand with a magic stick
Our forward line is bullet fast
And prefers to be last but one, if not last.
In football, we stand tall
And before the curtain rises, tend to fail.
In wrestling, we are a generous nation
And choose to lose so that others win.
Our legendary men in blue outfit.
Are so great that they'll never quit;
Their politics is so healthy and sound
That they can actually sleep on the ground
And with Sourav Ganguly in such great form
We are beyond defeat and harm.
In such a scenario of sporting glory
Sania Mirza and Anand Vishwanathan
Spoil our country's reputation
They should either stop winning
Or something against them should soon be done.

15.10.2005

Only Annihilation

I AM Osama bin Laden
And I live by the gun
Killing the 'infidels' of the world
Is a necessity and not a part of my fun.
My grain, my brain, my chain if you want to see
My concern for purity, my love of pious humanity,
My spirit, my grit, my moments of genuine fit,
If you want to see the fruit of the tree of religiosity,
The land of the chosen, the heaven on earth
If you want to meet by any chance the 14th century
If your journey on earth is of any worth
I invite you to Kabul,
I'll take you on a trip of Kandahar
Which we are saving,
We are at war, for jehad is the thing
The world is burning for it heeds not
Our philosophy, our advice, our thought;
It's our duty now to take it back to civilisation
The price of which is nothing much,
Only annihilation.

6.10.2001

Let There be Light

As Ravan goes up in flames
And Meghnath,
Kumbhkaran follow suit,
Jump and gyre, dance with the fire
For the demons have been given the boot.
The time has come to light the sky.
With smiles and laughter,
The time has come to love thy neighbour,
The time when joy will join labour
And the time for the death of the blood-sucker.
The time once again of the moon and the tide,
The time of the bashful bride,
The time for a country of a billion
To feel proud of being Indian,
The time when patriotism will once again hold sway,
And only the others race to the USA
So from abode to abode
Let the crackers explode
And fireworks fly
To light up the sky.

15.10.2001

The Poor Big B

(Canvassing for his then-favoured-political-party in the election to UP assembly in 2007)

Our beloved Big B
Must be living in poverty
Feted alike at home and abroad.
The poor man has to work very hard
Sell Reid and Taylor, sell for Dabur
Making their product look like gold
Making for them claims most bold.
A true workman without any qualms
He sells his name because his name is sold.
Our icon supreme is praising oil, promoting cream
And is now for U.P. going full steam.
Claiming that U.P.
mein hai dum kyunke jurm yahan hai kum
U.P. is great because it has a low crime rate
And Meerut and Nithari fall outside the state.

7.4.2007

Let the Children Take Over

They may not know economics, politics, diplomacy,
They may not be able to rewrite history,
They may not know how to pit street against street,
They may not be able to rend the sky with war cry,
They may not plan and execute a sly ambush,
They may not be able to make millions out of UTI,
They may not have perfected demagogy yet,
They may not be able to generate sufficient hatred,
They may ask for love and equality instead,
They may think, of happiness, laughter, play grounds,
They might commit the sin of innocence, idealism, honesty,
They might lisp, be playful and offend our ponderousness,
They might banish prejudice, prudery, even hypocrisy
They might outlaw war and harm arms industry,
And in this world, at home with anxiety,
Like birds, they might sing and dance
These risks are certainly there, but I think,
The children should be given a chance.

12.1.2002

Blessings of Being a Fool

'MY MOTHER is Nehru's sister
And Subhash Chandra Bose is my brother,
At my uncle's we supped last night at Teen Murti,
What a gracious host is Indiraji,
Pandit ji there, Patel and Lal Bahadur Shastri,
She hugged me, kissed me –
Lady Mountbatten,
Oh what fun!'
So switched on our friend Shankar Chaudhry
Who became a hakeem and earned thirty thousand a month
After he failed for the fifth time in his FSc
Free from all manner of manners,
Free with your fancy
If you can at will fast forward and rewind
You're the blessed bone of mankind.
Full of sound, and from sense if you're free,
If you can climb any tree,
Sit on top and cheer,
You're the man of the year.
If you laugh when people hoot you
And sing when they cry
And talk endlessly until they die,
If you have a relation present at every skirmish on the Indo-Pak border,

Boast of a shopping complex in Bombay and three houses in
Delhi,
As your friend buys you a cup of tea,
And tell everybody about the grand party you are going to
throw
If you don't know it, you had better know
That life can be wonderfully cool
If you are born one or can become a fool.

9.2.2012

DTC Ride

A YOUNG woman drops her tiffin and a gentleman falls on
his face
As they race for the approaching bus
A crowd that had waited patiently, peacefully, restlessly,
A crowd that a leader could easily use for a rally
Turns suddenly athletic
Elbowing, punching, pole-vaulting, kicking . Rubbing
intensely as the poor lady is squeezed, and sweats,
As the rest let out their spleen, curse and fight
As some of them laugh at her plight
And some with shirts torn and trousers down
Fume and frown;
Brick against brick, sack on sack, we have suffocation inside,
Scramble out, and a swelling footboard, and bedlam on the
road.
Hail my country, hail,
After half a century of freedom
While the public transport trips
And we ponder long and deep
We can feel proud that a family of three in Delhi
Can half a dozen cars keep.

11.5.2002

In the National Interest

(The politicians do everything in the "national interest.")

IN THE national interest, I climb your shoulders
In the national interest, I can jump from the sky
In the national interest, I have always lived
In the national interest, I can any day die.
In the national interest, I play ping pong
National interest is my theme song,
National interest is my war-cry,
So whatever I do never can be wrong,
For as long as I prosper the nation is strong.
From me what do you want more
The nation's future is secure,
For its sake, I have cleared the decks,
For its sake, I can change my name, party and sex.

27.5.2002

On Teacher's Day

A nation's fate, it should be clear even to a fool
Is fashioned in a school,
In a college or a university
Of which the teacher is the key.
But where is he
The teacher that used to be?
In any case, where is he or she
In the social hierarchy?
An object of pity,
Who'll like to marry off his daughter
To a mere master?
And when the society's curse
Makes him worse and worse
Is it not a small mercy
That COURTESY Radhakrishnan
He is remembered ritually
Once at least by the nation,

5.10.2001

Zareena

To put it plain and flat
She's a babysitter, and is paid for that.
Plain and flat, for she can often put on the mat
My jokes and go on with her work.
One of the siblings six or seven
Unschooled, unleashed on the market at eleven
She finds her slot, and I've often got
A taste of her mettle as she orders me out
Of the study to dust it clean.
Keen like a hawk, ever on her guard
To pounce upon you even if affectionately
You utter a word against her ward.
So zealous of the child, so playfully naughty
Uncontrollable as she laughs uproariously,
Hardly ever enquired after by her father
Utterly oblivious of her family,
Needling my sentimentality
About a son or a daughter,
Shouting and flitting from room to room,
I watch her and wonder,
A boss in my own house
Couldn't she be a master
At any counter,
This babysitter!
It's a democratic order, after all.

2.8.2002

Terror Tuesday

HORRIFYING, HORRENDOUS, terrible
The hounds of hell have struck too well,
The blasts of Bombay float thick and fast
Mere phantoms though, so at last
The world and the West know what it should have known
    long ago
That earthquake you reap if tremors you sow.
But no, their darlings still are precisely those
Who breed and feed and lead the hate campaign
Rain death and destruction, devastation and pain,
Precisely those who call terror the freedom struggle
And do in Washington what in Srinagar they have done.
Oh the mother of terror leads the anti-terror blast
Oh that shortsightedness should make the world's power so
    blind
That cure of terror in its cause it should find:
And root not out the poisonous plant,
Hatred and fanaticism, injustice and insanity;
And merely want the arrogance of money and power prevail
And buy up countries ever on sale.
As for us, if we look up to them, and not they to us,
If we think they'll warm our hearths and comfort deliver
Out in the cold cold night we'll shiver.

13.10.2003

Fanaticism and War

(When Kargil war was on)

I RISE every morning and pray to God
Give me wisdom, give me peace, O Lord
Give me patience, charity, tolerance
But above all, give me love, and give me the capacity
To see in everybody thy divine essence.
This is my religion, but with the rising sun
Most often
It turns into fanaticism, into bigotry blind
Where all other religions and the rest of mankind
Should be either thrown into the ocean,
Or placed before the gun.
But for this fanaticism, there would be no partition
But for this bigotry
Obviously,
Not this present war.

10.7.1999

Happy Birthday

Happy birthday to you, Bapu
Hundred and thirty today,
Dance and sing with us, pray
For the way you walked on
Has already become the nation's highway.
In all our personal intercourse
In every business deal
Whether we marry or divorce
Or sell onion or steel
We speak nothing but the truth;
Whether it is a state of war
Or elections in Bihar
Non-violence is our guiding spirit;
Snobbery, selfishness, guile and greed
Have from India disappeared indeed,
Inequalities are a thing of the past
And Dalits are in heaven at last,
Service before self is the politicians' aim
And national character is the name of the game.
Replacing the kings and queens on our currency notes
You have staged a virtual coup
Happy birthday to you.

2.10.1999

Beyond Man and God

(When the BMW which killed seven labourers sleeping on the pavement was sought to be made into a truck)

YOU CAN murder and you can rape
And take my word for it, you will escape scot-free
If the tree under which you stand
Has leaves of gold, and is manured with
power and perversity.
Wheel and deal or kill at will
You sons of the rich, go gaily amuck
And never for a moment bother
For I have discovered a simple device
That can turn a BMW into a truck.
Whether it is Tandoor or murder in the Inn
I guarantee, you will win.
Fear not dear, for the law is one of your in-laws
And those who enforce it know too well your worth,
Fear no power divine or terrestrial
For great God is asleep in heaven
And all is well with the earth.

18.10.1999

Rejoicing

I WILL roam freely in Pahlgam now
And sit alone by the vast Wular Lake,
Go skating at the Sonmurg glacier
And at Gulmurg cut my birthday cake.
In the hills of Banihal I would love to be
And have my heart's fill at the Dal and the Char Chinar,
Anantnag and Barinag haunt me day and night,
From visiting the Nishat I'll no longer myself bar.
I am a free man now with all my fears gone,
The fear of being killed or kidnapped in Kashmir is a fear in vain
Rejoice my soul, for in Srinagar now
I am no longer less safe than in a DTC bus
Or in an ordinary train,
Or, for that matter, in an Indian Airlines plane.

2.1.1999

Letter to Musharraf

DEAR GENERAL Musharraf,
I agree with your policy of bluster and bluff,
You have every right to spit fire
And into a bloody conflict mire
The subcontinent.
I understand your need to spread terrorism
Against a neighbour,
I understand my dear,
Your need to stay in power
As a dictator.
I understand your talk of a nuclear clash,
I understand your constant talk of a catastrophe
In which India will suffer grievously,
In which Pakistan will win gloriously
And for ever live prosperously,
But General, there is a possibility
That from the map of the world
Pakistan may cease to be,
But that of course is not your worry.
By the way, when are you visiting your
haveli in Delhi?

19.2.2006

Protest

(When there was a violent protest against Mira Nayar's 'water')

NOT A single woman is burnt for dowry
In my country
Nor is anyone molested in the office
There is just no nudity on our TV
And our films are absolutely pure culturally
Invasion of the foreign media
From the skies
Its obscenity and sexuality
Have been stopped entirely.
Khajuraho is not a part of our inheritance
Really.
Widows in my country
Are a proud species
They are especially invited
At every wedding or any other occasion
Of auspiciousness and festivity.
They are welcomed in every home with smiling faces
We are certainly not the asses
To persecute a mother or a daughter.
Therefore we protest 'Water'
As once earlier
We put out 'Fire'

11.3.2000

About our Women

(When a woman was paraded naked for marrying outside her caste)

GLORY BE to her! Is she ever
Paraded naked for marrying outside her caste
Or hanged by a tree for everyone to see
For being too fast?
Has a woman been ever called a witch?
Or has she been abused by the rich?
Has a widow been ever slighted?
Or an issueless woman in your knowledge blighted?
Has anyone been burnt for dowry?
Or beaten up at all?
Or when she gives birth to a female child
Does a woman even feel small?
Do you know how peacefully a single woman lives?
And the compliment her employer gives?
Not only in the days of queen Draupadi.
But even today, do you know
How worship of woman is a religion in our country?

15.6.2000

Metamorphosis of Dream Girl

(On Vyjayanthimala)

'TAN DOLE *mera* man dole, *mere dil ka gaya karar re*
Ab kaun bajaye bansuriya
Rings again in my ears
As I am thrown back by 50 years
And before my mind's eye, see
A spell-binding, eagle-eyed beauty.
That elegance again, that delicacy
The heart-throb of a whole generation then
That whirling dance, the wiry elasticity
Once again dancing before me I see
That mad, mad beauty.
The vision from Eden rose last night
When to my horror and fright
I saw Vyjayanthimala Bali
Defending the indefensible, pathetically embroiled
In the partisan Film Award controversy.
A spectre or what. . .! For god's sake ask me not
How looked she,
The death of a dream,
How I wish I had never seen
What I saw last night on the TV screen.

28.5.2001

Phoolan's Dying Statement

You call me a cold-blooded murderer
You paint me as a whore
You accuse me of amassing wealth
In your lexicon, I am uncouth vengeful dacoit and much
more.
I know, you resent my political ascendancy
I know, for you I am a butt of ridicule
I know, you are all men of decency
Full of righteous indignation, honour and honesty.
I know, your blood boils (doesn't it?) when women are
gangraped
I know, you feel like setting the world on fire
When the criminals have escaped
I know, when minor girls are bought and sold
Beaten blue and black for not being sexually bold
You are hurt in your heart so deep
That you forego your dinner and vow not to sleep
Isn't it?
The mother of all diseases and the enemy of decency
I know, you're uprooting poverty from this country,
Caste hierarchy, exploitation and cruelty.
And therefore found me guilty,
I know, why I have been murdered openly.

1.9.2001

Debt and a Death Trap

THOUGH A post-graduate from a premier university
Economics is not my cup of tea,
But when poetry fails and sentiments flounder
And "shared history" and "common culture"
On top of a crowd of cliches
Come a cropper,
It is only proper to plead
That the two countries bleed
From their nose, from their belly, from their knees
Because of the Kashmir disease.
Pakistan is caught in a debt, nay, a death trap
And India thirsts for drinking water,
That cold and hunger routinely slaughter
A quarter of their population
While defence, that is, offence tears their budget apart;
I don't know who is a patriot,
He who ensures a failed State
What *with jehadis, trishul* and hate,
Or those who even at a cost
Some magic evolve
And the mounting tension dissolve.

2.7.2001

The Price of a Bride

Alongwith a pretty-looking bride
They gave him a Mercedes to ride –
And the bride's father being the community's king
They gave every *barati* a diamond ring
Two and a half crore was the total bill
But more was demanded still.
And more was paid, till ultimately
The one-year-old bubbling bride
Hanged herself, and justified
The wide-spread practice of female foeticide.

28.4.2008

Bhopal Tragedy

(When there was a demand for higher compensation to the victims of Bhopal and action against Anderson, the Union Carbide Chairman)

Merely for filling the air of Bhopal with poison
And taking the lives of a few thousand men, women and
children;
The cops first arrested Warren Anderson;
Which was a heinously wrongful action;
And now we have raked up the case again;
And given the gentleman unnecessary pain;
Forgive, O Lord, the ex-Collector of Bhopal and others;
Who know not how much prosperity Union Carbide has
brought;
How much misunderstanding the latest revelation creates;
And slurs the fair name of United States;
How unfair it is to certain Indian gentlemen;
Who might have expedited the escape of Anderson;
And possibly made a few millions or a billion;
And all this for the death of Indian men, women and
children;
Surely, we must not irritate Union Carbide and Mr
Anderson;
For suggesting a solution to India's over population.

7.4.2010

Ramblings

We have controlled population growth
And checked the price rise
Which are now touching the lower skies
Amit Shah is innocent, and his very look shows
That he cannot kill a couple of flies
Parliament functions normally
And away from all business shies
Ms Mamata Banerjee is a great Railway Minister
Who from the maidan in Kolkata cries
"You the people of Delhi, Mumbai and Chennai
Very safe in my hands your life lies
But let me first, with some help from Naxalites
To the chief ministership of Bengal rise;"
Bhishm Pitamah of the country K, Karunanidhi
Will see to it before he dies
That for seven generations in his family
Every child a minister's chair occupies;
And true to the maxim that there is lull before the storm
Rather dormant behan Mayawati lies;
So I can say on oath
That in political morality and service to the people
Our netas have touched the point of highest growth.

11.9.2010

The Guilty Doctor

(When Dr. Vinayak Sen was hauled up for his alleged links with ultras)

We have the greatest respect for our judiciary
Not just for the justice done but also its travesty
Hence the butchers of nineteen eighty four roam free
And the murderers of Gujarat have boundless glee
While a doctor who looks after the health of the tribals and
downtrodden,
Whose services make him one in a million
Is a guilty man of the nation.
Against our great nation, he waged a fight
For, whatever the police says must be right
So he should get a taste of this country's might,
While the scamsters and swindlers, for their brilliant record
Should never be held guilty of fraud
And because our judiciary can never fail
Dr Sen will remain in jail.

5.1.11

Sorry, Dear Kanimozhi

A smiling lady, sweet and pretty
A lady whose first love was poetry
And who entered politics most reluctantly,
My heart goes out naturally for Kanimozhi.
And the credit for this will go to K Karunanidhi,
Who was keen to see
That every member of his multi-branched family
Would serve the state or the country
That every member down to the eighth generation
Would be used for wealth creation
By occupying a position of power in the nation,
Of course, Karunanidhi had nothing to do with 2G
Or KalaignarTV
So in the Tamil Nadu elections he could distribute no money
Or give the voters anything free.
He was never a part of the 2G fraud
Oh God, until their fingers they have burnt
Have the old men ever anything learnt

12.3.2011

Osama and Pakistan

An apostle of goodness, in the service of human race
A picture of grandeur, glory and grace
It is being said, Osama is dead
And the rumour is being spread
That Pakistan is in the face, red
Whereas a father-figure of terror
Osama allegedly a mass murderer
An idea personified, was not meant for death.
And Pakistan has its commitment against terror shown
And in the estimation of the world grown
By perfecting the art of double-speak
With a straight face and footwork sleek.
May the truth forever shine in the
Pakistani state
And long live Osama the great.

2.5.2011

Murder or Suicide ?

(On the death of another medical officer in the infamous scam in the health department in U.P.)

He is the third top medical officer to have died
But since what the UP Government says cannot be denied
Dr Y.S. Sachan committed suicide.
In view of the "ideal" law and order situation in the state;
The courts or the CBI cannot otherwise decide.
"Abide by the highest standards of probity;"
Is by personal example taught by Mayawati;
So not only in the Health Department
A scam of three thousand crore in UP
Just cannot be;
No murder can take place
No criminal can escape
In UP, have you ever heard of rape?
No laws are violated; and the farmers agitation
Or criticism about Noida
Authority's land acquisition;
Is a ploy to defame Mayawati;
Because the whole world knows that UP
Is the paradise of this country.

19.8.2011

In Praise of Our Police

(The context of the poem is
Nithari child-abuse and killings)

I have a burning desire to praise the police,
Praise their policy never to harass or fleece,
Praise their courtesy, urgency, honesty,
Praise their impartiality and integrity,
Their resolve that justice must be done
And their practice not to accept money from anyone.
You and I have known them very well though
Their work in Noida was outstanding, even so;
No bones or skulls had they seen
And everything to them being clear as daylight,
No FIR could they write.
So they accused and abused those who came to complain
And asked them never to produce children again;
So, in vain is CBI digging the drain
And causing our policemen un-necessary pain
For, our police is snow-white clean –
And anybody who accuses them is either corrupt or mean.

Requiem to Sabharwal

(When Professor Sabharwal was beaten to death by a student body in Madhya Pradesh, 2006)

FULL of brilliance, culture and foresight,
Our youth being brave and full of fight
The future of India is really bright.
Only occasionally, they murder their teacher
Normally, they only break furniture
They hold up traffic, fold up classes
They would like to be political leaders, corporate bosses
They must have money and fun
So, what if they have to use the gun
For, the election to the Union must be won.
They are inventive, enterprising and bright
Instant stardom is their right,
So well-behaved they are, such pictures of courtesy
Because our society
Teaches them mercy, manners and morality,
They're so peace-loving, patriotic, free from guile
Because we set such brilliant examples all the while,
So, we should be proud of what we have done
Because they are our, our very own children.

6.10.2006

Pay Hike for the MPs

They too have a right to life, they too have a family to feed
Our MPs deserve a pay hike indeed
Because the principle is
To all according to their work, to
each according to his need,
First work; They have to sweat, fret and frown
They have to shout the Speaker down.
They have to run into the well,
And turn the House into a hottest hell.
They have to walk out and walk in the sun.
And every day march to the Rashtra-pati Bhavan
And most importantly, they have to ensure
That no work gets done.
Their motto being service to the people,
For themselves, they need not a thing
But people mustn't be ungrateful
And must pay for them to live like a king;
And then, they are entirely corruption-free,
So they deserve a big raise in salary.

3.9.2006

God and Gujrat

(The earthquake in Gujrat)

GOD IS in heaven and all is well with the world.
Only sometimes a few thousand houses collapse
Because they stand proud and tall,
Only sometimes a few thousand children die.
Because they're so innocent, so small
And because god loves them all.
When a wall crashes against a wall
And on our heads the roofs fall,
When the earth opens its belly
And gobbles up a whole city,
When a town turns into debris
Crushing underneath a chunk of humanity
Praise be to the almighty,
Praise be to his love and pity,
This earthquake is a guarantee
That god is in heaven and all is well with the world.

Ode to Janata Dal

(Running feud among Janata Dal constituents which then (1998) included Lalu Yadav, Sharad Yadav, Nitish Kumar, Navin Patnaik, Dev Gowda and the then Prime Minister Inder Kumar Gujral)

I sometime indulge the Janata Dal
For its proceedings are never dull:
With social justice, the avowed aim
And thumping of thighs, its favourite game,
With Hegde exiled, Gowda, the King
With Sharad and Laloo jumping in the ring
With Gujral and Dandavate silently looking;
Like in Karnataka, with daily jolt
With Biju's son in total revolt,
With a tide to ride, with a man on top
O welcome them for what they have done
Haven't they provided enough fun?

28.2.1998

Farmer's Suicides

A wonderful escape route had Punjab and Andhra shown
Every eight hours a farmer kills himself in Vidarbha alone
So that his debt may also be cremated along with his body.
Our GDP is growing at a break-neck speed
Our Sensex is at its peak, indeed
And we don't have food enough for our people to feed!
We are going to be a super-power in two thousand twenty
And our farmers are committing suicides,
Hourly regularly, daily!
It's an age of prosperity and plenty
A golden age of globalisation
So why should we mind a few thousand deaths by starvation!
And since we are so proud of our peasantry
They should naturally die for the country.

11.11.2006

City of the Commonwealth

Delhi is becoming a world-class city
And it's a pity
That the middle classes and the poor should cry
When the tax burden becomes unbearably high
They cry when the transport becomes costly,
They hate to pay more for the LPG and look at that
They resent even the increase in VAT
Already, they say, there is crushing inflation,
They forget that in the near future there is no election
They forget that to live in a world-class city
They should learn to do without milk, sugar and tea
Now Delhi is a place only for the super rich
And the upper middle class, from which
The rest should recite Ram naam, and go
And happily watch the Commonwealth show.

30.5.2010

Mayor of Gorakhpur

(When a eunuch became Mayor of Gorakhpur)

WITH THEIR hands raised chin-high
And songs rending the sky
They clap as their bodies sway
With the crowds hilarious and gay
Dancing behind them through the city
Drunk with the wine of victory
Asha Devi, the first hijra mayor of UP
Has announced to mobilise his or her biradri
To take over the reins of governance,
To, as the soothsayers say
Replace the NDA.
In the first instance, they'll contest
All the Assembly seats in UP.
To make the state civilised and great.
From there the light will spread to the rest of the country.
The golden age, or at the very least
The age of gender equality
Is close-by, courtesy Gorakhpur
That has made to the country its greatest contribution
After Firaq Gorakhpuri.

12.2.2005

To General Musharraf

"WHEN ARE you visiting your haveli in Delhi?"
I wrote to you last year, to which naturally
You couldn't reply.
But now as Vajpayee invites you, and you are arriving today
The news is that your locality
Is in full flow, abuzz and aglow
With faces and floodlight and unhidden pride,
And, like when they decorate an old hag,
They have redone your haveli into a bride
For you to embrace its loveliness and grace,
For this little space can squeeze into its size
The small hope and vast aspirations
Of the two nations
Which are one at least in grinding poverty,
More ancient and mighty
Than our perverse hostility.
Who knows it better than you?
And still you'll do what you'll do
But the two (of us) must know
That hatred and bigotry in their thrust
Always swallow up, their host first.
Be it as it is, so be it
Nothing much may come out of your visit
But if you visit your haveli, you'll see

How even over deviousness and insanity
Triumphs common humanity.
And if you agree, take at least this
Back with you and for your country.

15.9.2001

Musharraf and Jehad

(When there was an attempt at Musharraf's life)

"I AM riding a tiger, how do I dismount,
And count my dead and wounded!
The lid is off, I am clever by half
As the world knows how goes the world with me.
Indeed, my *jehadi* deeds bleed me.
Whichever way I go is hell
Hell bent as India seems to be to call my bluff
Even this brat Abdullah talks tough.
And if the weather continues to be rough
Yonder all before me I see
From Rawalpindi to Karachi
Deserts and devastated humanity
And the dustbin of history.
And if I act honestly
Against my conscience, against my conviction,
If I act against the monster,
It will devour me surely.
Oh my duplicity! O long live my duplicity,
Bush is still friendly
I can mislead still half the world
And my guest Bin Laden says
He can still bend the Statue of Liberty.
Let it be, let it be
In the meantime, I'll go and see Vajpayee on TV"

26.6.2002

Ode to Jayalalitha

(Jayalalitha was alleged to have spent a lot of money on the marriage of her "foster son".
She had at that time joined B.J.P. at the centre.)

THE tigress once again roars
She never spent a hundred crores
On the marriage of her foster-son:
It was all in the form of gifts,
And, thus, the truth from lies she sifts;
She is totally corruption-free
Therefore, she aligns with BJP

14.2.1998

Ode to Lalu

(The background is the infamous 'fodder scam'
which saw Lalu behind bars)

It's not a fairy tale
Lalu has, indeed, come out of jail
The prince, as usual, witty and calm
Forges an alliance with Kanshi Ram
Full cry in the election hunt
To defeat all including the United Front
And propagate the kindered breed
Who can with him on fodder feed
And, thus lead the nation with glee
Into the twenty first century.

14.2.1998

Take it, Mr. Gandhi

IT MAY not be your fault
That Surat had the worst plague of the century,
It may or may not be your fault
That worst earthquake should hit Gujarat,
But it's definitely your fault, Mr Gandhi
That the worst communal frenzy should visit your state repeatedly
That man should turn monster and burn fellow men,
Swing and sloganeer as they are roasted alive,
Make a bonfire of a whole railway compartment
And let no one survive,
Sprinkle petrol on a neighbour's body
And set it alight
Burn shops and houses, shanties and shrine
To demonstrate his might,
Fight as he loots a shoe shop,
Seal a whole village and set it ablaze
As children raise heart-rending (or heart-warming) cries
As the State tells threadbare lies.
It was very selfish of you Mr Gandhi
To take away with you all compassion, kindness, humanity,
To leave behind no non-violence, truth, tolerance,
And hence you are to blame for our insolvency
Can you for a day come to Gujarat and see, *prithee!*

6.4.2002

Parliament in Action

CUSTODIANS OF the nation, its conscience keepers
People's servants, faithful, well-wishers,
We stir, we stride, we run
Around in the House
Like the cat and the mouse
And provide you with all the fun
You need and indeed
When we shout and growl and yell,
Particularly when we squat in the well
We are at our brightest
And serve the nation best.
It is a mere few crores a day
That you have to pay
For us to dig out the truth;
But somehow
If you don't like our show
Ask those who rule now
How very much Parliament remained calm
When the issue was our, now their, Sukh Ram.

17.4.1999

Gandhi is Glad

(On the violence against Christians)

WELL DONE, my sons
Burn the churches, attack the nuns
Swell your cheeks and thump your chest
That is the answer to conversions.
I am sorry, all my life
I preached truth, preached non-violence
Foolishly preached religious tolerance,
Fasted for peace and vainly died.
But I am glad now to see you triumph
Glad to see your sense of pride.
Keep up the good work, my dear sons
And let this in my home be done,
In fundamentalism and bigotry
Let us second to no one be,
Emulate the greatest in the field
And push back this country
Like our neighbour
Into the fourteenth century.

30.1.1998

Demonstrating in Underwears

(When the activists of a political party demonstrated outside some people's houses in 1999)

OUR COUTURE is our culture
And it is for us to decide, Sir
What it is, what it ought to be, and what it is not;
It is none of anybody's business
To debate, question or even to discuss
And, thus, hurt us
We'll break into the house, pull down posters and
    burn the theatre
And in particular
Since we believe in democracy, free expression and
    people's order
Our dear Dilip Kumar, Shabana Azmi, Javed Akhtar
You have seen us in our underwears
But remember
Even these underwears are not for ever

2.1.1999

Hypocrisy is My Name

(When America put pressure on India to sign C.T.B.T.)

I can bomb and I can blast
The cities and towns as I feel
There should be some order in the world
So I have to keep it under my heel.
I stifle nations and throw their scientists out
For I stand for prosperity, everywhere
And also because I stand for peace, I kill
All those who dare oppose my will.
My bright face, if you want to see
Go to Vietnam, Hiroshima, Nagasaki,
I want the world to be nuclear-free.
My own stockpiles? Silly!
I want you to sign C.T.B.T.

Clinton Speaking

(On Clinton Levensiky affair)

I am the President of U.S.A.
And why should you bother if I am a little gay?
On my shoulders lies the burden of the globe
So what if the secrets of a staffer's body
Sometimes I probe
I am not a cow-boy, on oath I say
I am truthful man, not guilty of perjury
Let the asses bray as they may
I have on my side, my wife, Hillary,
And finally, this is my plea:
It was she who had an affair with me
I had nothing to do with Levinsky.

Homeless in Winter

Against the icy winds and the bone-chilling cold
When the skies are freezing or frozen
When under the blanket or quilt we shiver
And need a hot beverage every hour
They sleep in the open
Because it is a lot of fun
On the pavements and roadsides of the city
Rows upon rows you see
Obviously, sleeping most peacefully!
They come to the hospital
Bewildered and aghast
And bear the wintry blast,
And because of cold
Not lack of treatment
Breathe their last.
Not only a nation great
We are a welfare state
A land of equality and plenty
Where starvation is a thing of the times old
And nobody can die of cold

18.3.2012

Age of Austerity

Full page pictures of Ambedkar and Rajiv Gandhi
On their birth and death anniversary
Costing crores to the country
Are indeed an example of austerity,
Which in this dire economic scenario
Is a crying necessity.
Six thousand guests at a marriage reception
Of the son of a businessman or a politician
And piles of food rotting in the morning
Showcase the warfooting
On which we are practicing frugality!
Fleets of Cars choking the city
Ten-acre farmhouses hosting late night parties
Mirror not only the economic situation in the country
But also establish an identity
With the vast majority living in poverty!
And finally, business executives with ten crores of annual
salary
Have of necessity to practise frugality,
While with their sandals and jewellery respectively
Two shining examples of austerity
Are Jayalalitha and Mayawati.

3.7.2012

Inflation

Fruits and pulses, rice and ghee
Vegetables and flour, sugar and tea
Were once upon a time in greater
or smaller measure
Used by everybody
In a certain country.
The farmers were happy
And the consumers felt easy.
And then, a species called blackmarketeer
and hoarder
And their cousin forward trader
And airy-fairy wealth producer
In the name of economy, free
Took over the country —
Leaving behind only a sweet memory.

24.4.2008

Hike in Power Tariff

In this season of sweltering heat
My dear wife and children sweet
I hope you will not mind
If I leave a few tips behind:
It is much better to brood in the pitch dark night
Than switching on your bed-room light,
Learn to sweat out like a stoic most patiently
Rather than switch on the cooler or A.C
Go and sit under a shady neighbourhood tree
And revive the ancient culture of your country
And finally to conclude this part of my will
Keep by your bed-side a strong sleeping pill
And avoid running up a hefty power bill
For, whether it is the beginning of the month,
 middle or the start
You ought to be stingy and smart
For, balancing the household budged has become
 a rare fine art.

3.4.1999

The Pulse of Our Times

'The Pulse of Our Times' is a rigourous selection from more than four hundred poems published over fifteen years in the leading newspapers and journals of the country. Wit, satire and humour are their defining features.

Arrogance and hypocrisy are today the hallmark of the powers that be and corruption and scams have become their driving force. These are treated here with subtle irony and humour. These poems give a synoptic overview of the socio-political scene of the country today. Beside satirical pieces, the collection has heart-warming poems of love and on personal relations, as also peoms of inspiration and about people who have made a mark and won our love and admiration:

I stand up sky-high and salute the human spirit,
Its limitlessness, its might, its grit,
The mind of man I sing
As I salute Stephen Hawking.

Learn to be happy, learn to clap
Even when your son gives you a slap,
And if you are way laid by a robber
Salute him and quietly surrender
Form in this media age
In this age of road rage
For, in this age of soaring voilence
Even saving our life is an offence
Only your importance is your defence.

Kuldip Salil has published five volumes of poetry. He has translated Mir, Ghalib, Faiz, Iqbal, Ahmad Faraz and other Urdu poets into English verse and a book of best-known English poems into Hindi poetry and won accolades for these translations including Sahitya Akademi award. He retired as Associate Professor of English from Hans Raj Collage, University of Delhi.